A book is a treasure we keep in our memory chest...
this treasure belongs to:

_____

To My Beloved, Who Was The Light of Day

Composed in the United States of America
Printed in Seoul, Korea

First Impression 2006
ISBN 0-9777340-1-3
SAN: 850-637X

Library of Congress Cataloging-in-Publication Data

Carman, Debby
Purrlonia's Lullaby / written and illustrated by Debby Carman

Summary: 1. Cats - Fiction   2. Friendship   3. Rhyming Stories
I. Carman, Debby, ill.   II. Carman, Debby   III. Purrlonia's Lullaby

Purrlonia's Lullaby

A parable written and illustrated by Debby Carman©

Would you like to meet a darling cat,
One who charms the mice and can tame a rat?

Her purr is like a lullaby,
From a music box that resides inside

Her coat is made of velvet down,
Soft as feathers ever found

She hums a note and then a tune,
Enticing bees to swarm and swoon

Purrlonia hums a lullaby,
The birds take flight and soar on high

How does she attract such keen attention,
This cat that purrs in a new dimension?

"The music comes from within my heart,
Suddenly the purr machine will start"

Attracting snails to slide up close,
The music comes, the music goes

But in the process no one knows

How does she attract such keen attention,
This cat that purrs in a new dimension?

Purrlonia sat on her velvet down,
Purrlonia gathered her friends around

Together were bees buzzing by mice,

Strutting were stinkbugs,
Trying to be nice!

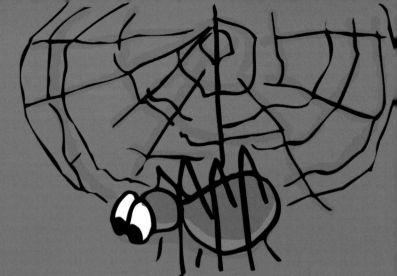

A spider was dangling
from high by a thread

Hovering were hummingbirds near overhead

Perched were the blue jays —
warbling a song

While slinky long caterpillars wiggled along

How does she attract such keen attention,
This cat that purrs in a new dimension?

"The music comes from within my heart,
Suddenly the purr machine will start"

Purrlonia's hope was to be a friend,
And purrmurring is the message she sends

Purring was her exceptional feature,
Her desire was to connect with each creature

"We are all connected by threads and by strings,
We are all affected by the very same things"

"We are all precious and unique each one
No one is better or more special, not one"

How does she attract such keen attention,
This cat that purrs in a new dimension?

"I have a song, a purr melody,
A murmur, a purrmurr, a pure harmony"

"Each of us has a close connection,
We survive and thrive
through mutual protection"

"To protect and to preserve,
Is what we all deserve"

Purrlonia's purrmurring a lullaby.

The End